A

MW00719802

A VERY STRANGE
CHRISTMAS!

Anton Von Stefan

GRANVILLE ISLAND
PUBLISHING

Copyright © 2020 Anton Von Stefan

All rights reserved. No part of this publication may be reproduced, stored in a retrieval system or transmitted, in any form or by any means, without prior permission of the publisher or, in the case of photocopying or other reprographic copying, a license from Access Copyright, the Canadian Copyright Licensing Agency, www.accesscopyright.ca, 1-800-893-5777, info@access copyright.ca.

Publisher's Cataloging-in-Publication Data

Names: Von Stefan, Anton, author.
Title: A Very strange Christmas! / Anton Von Stefan.
Description: Vancouver, BC: Granville Island Publishing, 2019.
Identifiers: ISBN 9781989467152
Subjects: LCSH Christmas—Fiction. | England—Fiction. |
Criminals—Fiction. | Poverty—Fiction. | Conduct of life—
Fiction. | Short stories, Canadian. | BISAC FICTION / Short
Stories | FICTION / Holidays
Classification: LCC PR9199.3 .V65 V47 2019 |
DDC 813.6—dc23
Ebook ISBN: 978-1-989467-17-6

Editor: Kyle Hawke
Book designer: Omar Gallegos
Proofreader: Rebecca Coates

Photo on cover by Florian Olivo

Granville Island Publishing Ltd.
212 – 1656 Duranleau St. Granville Island
Vancouver, BC, Canada V6H 3S4

604-688-0320 / 1-877-688-0320
info@granvilleislandpublishing.com
www.granvilleislandpublishing.com

Printed in Canada on recycled paper

*I dedicate this book to my brother, Olaf,
and my sister-in-law, Helga, who,
through their kindness, brought this book
to a much earlier publication date.*

Acknowledgements

This book came to the forefront in my drive to have a second book published through my introduction to Tom Middler, a member of Open House Theatre, Vienna, Austria. Without that encounter, a meeting which took place after seeing his latest stage rendition of *A Christmas Carol* by Charles Dickens, my book *A Very Strange Christmas!* would have been published a few years down the road.

I owe many people thanks for their encouragement to continue with my drive to publish: Olaf and Helga, my brother and sister-in-law, who took me to that play in December of 2018. Irene McKinney, who set me on the right course toward the proper use of the English language. Mary Jean Dunsdon (Watermelon), a very good friend, and Gerard Mahony in Vancouver, for their continued support. George Oberländer in Bobcaygeon, Ontario, whose testimonial prophesied the publication. Finally, Elizabeth Elwood of the Vagabond Players, New

Westminster, whose plays inspired me to complete this book within its time frame.

I wish to thank Jolena Hope, Tamara Gorin, Dianne Ganz, and Becky Matheson in British Columbia; Rose Travis in Primrose, Ontario; Mary Norrad in Sussex, New Brunswick; Diane Burden in Tennycape, Nova Scotia; thanks to Mary Lamb for their support in Canada.

Internationally, a huge thanks to Sheila Perlaki from Shakespeare & Company and Felicitas Lang, Canadian Embassy, Vienna, Austria.

Imaginary scenarios were run by Larry and Betty Walker as well as Bruce and Shannon Chadwick. From our long-term acquaintance I borrowed a name or two for the characters.

Posthumously, I must mention my mother, Mathide, who through her artwork inspired me to write this Christmas story.

To my publisher, Jo Blackmore; my editor, Kyle Hawke; the book's designer, Omar Gallegos; and for her technical expertise on the work for the cover image, Shannon. Thanks for believing in me.

— Anton Von Stefan

Each year just before Christmas, on the 24th day of December to be exact, in one of the poorest neighbourhoods in the old town in which we live, there would come this gentleman, often accompanied by his good wife, to a particular square where a rather sizeable fire had been lit.

That fire would burn brightly within a discarded forty-five-gallon oil drum, its sole purpose to keep those in its vicinity warm. Those close by would sit upon meagre bundles, an old suitcase, a wooden crate, a discarded keg, or any other item one happened to possess, attempting to absorb as much of the heat as possible.

Once the gentleman had arrived and word had spread through the community, those further off would come out of their makeshift homes, places of refuge often within the alleyways of the district. In fact, any abandoned place which afforded some comfort against the cold and the wind was a carefully guarded piece of real estate the poor people didn't easily abandon. Yet, on that particular night, an exception was made. A few of these individuals carried twigs, pieces of wood, or anything that would likely burn and which could be added to that fire as the night waned, to replenish its glow and its warmth.

The gentleman at the heart of this story was not overly dressed for the time of year or the hour of day, but his attire did make him stand out slightly amidst the people and the district he chose to visit. He seldom wore a hat, usually displaying a thick crop of well-groomed shoulder-length greying hair. This colour was matched in a short-trimmed beard which covered most of his exposed face and upper lip. A thin nose, which from its appearance may once have been broken, separated the space between his two grey-green eyes and presented a kind expression.

From the first time I ever laid eyes upon him, he was already an older fellow, the wrinkles on his forehead attesting to this fact. Yet — I must be clear — in all the years he came by our part of the city, I cannot recall that he ever aged.

Unquestionably, once we gathered round and he began to speak, the air would become quite still and not a single person would cough or stir lest we miss even a single word of the story this gentleman told. Should snow begin to fall, as was often the case on the 24th of December back then, we would bundle ourselves up a little more and sit closer together, but in all of those years, not a single person ever left until the last words were spoken.

"Many years ago . . . ," the slim and rather tall gentleman would begin, a jovial smile spreading across his weathered and rosy face while a kind twinkle was evident in his eyes.

Before adding to those introductory words, however, he'd cast his gaze upon one and all. Taking his time to scan the crowd, he would look upon each individual in their turn. Only when he was content that all appeared as comfortable as possible would he continue.

Yes, it was some years back, in this very town, upon this very night, and in close proximity to this exact square of this particular neighbourhood that a remarkable set of events began to unfold which would forever alter the lives of all the people it touched.

Now before I go much further, and for those of you who are about to hear my tale for the first time, I need to tell you about the man at the centre of this story. For the moment, I shall refer to him only as Kenneth, his Christian name.

As it was Christmas Eve, Kenneth had already passed his birthday, a date which fell on the 12th of December, and so he was a few days over thirty-one when these strange events took place. He was not what you and I would call a gentleman, but he was not so black at heart that you would call him a highwayman either.

He was a man who had parents, much like all of you children here in our midst . . .

Here, the jolly storyteller would use one of his hands to point at the many faces of the young children who surrounded him. Their small noses had long ago turned red from the cold, and the flickering light from the fire reflected off their tender skin, amplifying that crimson colour.

Kenneth had both a father and a mother. Of course, we all do at some time in our lives. Without parents, there would be no children, no families, and little hope for our future.

His father was never a steady wage-earner and you could well say that Kenneth was born into a rather poor family. When you add that his father had a fancy for beer and wine and that this affection became his undoing, often resulting in his loss of employment, life at home was not as ideal a place as it might have been.

His mother had been quite the opposite, poor soul, but she died when Kenneth was about five weeks past his ninth birthday. She had her heart in the right place and worked long hours as a seamstress. Above all, she was a pious woman. I cannot recall a single Sunday whereupon she did not attend church, often dragging her young son along for the service.

Kenneth's father, however, only went to church twice while that man was alive: once on his wedding day, the other to attend his wife's funeral.

At this point, the storyteller, who stood amongst the spellbound crowd, would wave to those who had recently arrived and were further back.

"Come on up to the fire and keep warm," he would say. "Out there, if I were to whisper, you may well miss a word or two, and you wouldn't want that, now would you?"

Once everyone had moved closer to where the gentleman stood, he would continue.

Although much shorter than her husband, Kenneth's mother was not one with which to trifle. The few small rooms they rented were her domain, and she often stood up to the almost penniless, besotted man who would stagger through the door after a night at Mahony's Irish Bar.

On those occasions, Kenneth would hide in the bedroom closet. He was too small to prevent what occurred and did not wish to witness the domestic violence which often followed that kind of arrival. Yet, on more than one occasion, he had seen his mother repeatedly strike his father with her open hand, a wooden soup spoon, or whatever utensil she happened to have at hand. Despite their physical difference and the threat of any aggression from his father, she would fly into a rage the moment he stepped over the threshold, the screaming increasing as an already dire situation became more extreme.

Those heated words, spoken in anger and bearing little weight on the love she held for his father, could not be expunged by placing his small hands over his ears. Most of the time, as he crouched in that closet, Kenneth closed his eyes and began to softly cry in a vain effort to distance himself from the violent action which took place. Like most little children, we all believe we can become invisible when we shut our eyes to the world outside. It is the magic of youth, and I shall not dispel that idea — God forbid!

The narrator stressed this last particular point.

Those unforgettable nights were to shape Kenneth's future. While his mother was still alive, they would usually end with his father finally breaking down and sobbing in shame while he asked for forgiveness. Shortly thereafter, the fighting would end, but the atmosphere within the home would be anything but pleasant for the remainder of the evening.

The gentleman who held the crowd's attention would then stop relating his tale. He would seem to reflect upon some memory which saddened his face for an instant, then the smile would reappear and he would continue.

Kenneth had two brothers. One was already fifteen when Kenneth was born. That older sibling had been apprenticed as a boilermaker by the time Kenneth could walk. The other was only five years older than Kenneth and left home three years after their mother's passing. There had been an older sister between the two older brothers, but she had been born prematurely and had died just twenty-seven days after her birth. He was not aware of any stone marker or grave, which, without doubt, his mother would have visited. As it was, only on a rare occasion would he ever hear his mother mention his sister, and that was usually in a hushed prayer while they were in church.

Three years after his mother's death, when his older brother ran off to make his own way in the world, Kenneth's life began the downward spiral which placed him out on the street on the Christmas Eve of this tale.

Without his mother, school was no longer much of a priority; his father couldn't have cared less if he attended classes or failed. Before he was ten, Kenneth dropped out of school. Restless and without parental guidance, he soon fell in with a group of youths who worked the streets under the leadership of an aged thief, a Fagin if you will. Yet, even this kind of camaraderie was not a life which suited the youth, and he soon broke out on his own. He idled his time away, taking on odd jobs here and there.

At first, he did well enough, especially in the summer. In the first two years after dropping out of school, he enjoyed picking blueberries, and as he grew older, he discovered there was better pay gathering strawberries at the farms surrounding the town. In the winter months, as the jobs vanished with the end of the harvest and the cold winds descended from the north, he often felt pangs of hunger and the need for shelter.

His first transgression of the law which placed him in front of a magistrate was indeed driven by hunger, a feeling I am sad to say many of you experience on a daily basis.

At this point in his story, the jolly man at the centre of the haggard crowd would stretch himself and shake off the snow which had accumulated upon his head and the shoulders of his coat. Then, he would sit down and continue to relate his story.

Hunger gnaws at our stomachs, its pangs bring on headaches, and those constant cravings seem to affect our very bones. As days go by without any real nourishment, that pain only intensifies, becoming a constant reminder which eventually overpowers all other thought. If opportunity knocks, it will drive a person to steal in an attempt to satisfy that craving.

During the day, if a situation presented itself, Kenneth honed his pickpocketing skills. At night, he began to break into abandoned sheds and small warehouses. At times, he even entered private residences when the timing was right. Yet, in all the years in which he had bolstered his income through those nefarious acts, he was never a violent man. If caught in the act, he would run, preferring to remain anonymous and at large rather than accost anyone. Yet, the dire situation Kenneth often found himself in was not solely of his own doing.

It was usual for the narrator to pause when he would come to this part of his tale. Once more, his demeanour would wane and sadness would seem to sweep over his face. For a moment, he would look down to the ground while pondering some distant thought. Often, a few of those listening would rise and either stoke the fire or add some wood to replenish it. Then, as the gentleman's smile returned, he would look up at those around him and continue with the story.

This town, like so many others, had factories which used to provide work. Yet, the meagre wages paid for that labour had many of us still trying to make ends meet, living from one paycheque to the next. For many of us back then, Christmas shopping was a last-minute affair accomplished just after we received our paycheques late in December. When the economy crashed in 1929, there was little demand for the products our hands produced and fewer shifts were required. One person after another found themselves without work. In the end, even a single shift on the production line was no longer required.

In the years which followed, the working class suffered most. Yet, clerks, bank tellers, and small shop owners also joined the ranks of the unemployed. Tens of thousands of layoffs resulted as the economy suffered from the stock market's crash. Hapless folk, much like everyone here, had little hope of being rehired. The Christmas of 1932 was no banner year for business, and it was in that particular year, on the evening of December 24th, that Kenneth found himself out on the street.

It was the night before Christmas and Kenneth had not managed to score in well over a week. He was plumb out of money and out on the prowl. There was no use staying on his side of the tracks.

Oh, that town had a makeup much like this town and so many others. The poorer neighbourhood was east of a narrow river which lazily wound through the small city, effectively cutting it in two. The western bank held the business section, or what was left of it. The wealthy lived west of that economic heart, on a hilly area overlooking the business district and the river. Around Christmas, the residences of the well-to-do were seldom, if ever, closed up long enough for him to make a visit and ply his trade.

East of the river's bank was the mainstream of the town's population. In the late 19th Century, with the expansion of the steam locomotive's territory, a railway was built on that side of the river, set well away from the river's bank to the east. Its arrival also split the eastern side of the city in half. East of those iron rails, where the poorer people had settled, many of the tenants were evicted as homeowners sold their property to make way for the industrialisation which was to follow. Yet, Cameron Lane, Courtney's Lair, and a few other dilapidated residential

areas somehow survived. These pitiful
communities lay just east of that
industrial area, almost forgotten even
by the town's middle and lower classes.

Cameron Lane had been built
prior to industry's arrival and was as
far from the town's heart as you can
imagine. Courtney's Lair had initially
been constructed as temporary hous-
ing for the workers who had been
employed in the factories. Now that
most of that industry lay abandoned,
it was a forlorn place which housed
only those families who had nowhere
else to live. Kenneth knew that visiting
that part of town would not help with
his financial situation, one he wished
to resolve.

On the day in question, snow
began falling shortly before noon. By
evening, it was coming down quite
rapidly, and with the temperature well
below freezing, the flakes were small
and easily shifted with a passing wind.
On that Christmas Eve, it was blowing
harder than usual and the snow was
being pushed about in a lively way,
rapidly drifting upon the flowing
currents of air. This resulted in small

whirlwinds within which it was almost impossible to see. Kenneth's spirits rose. The lack of visibility and the oncoming darkness would only help him evade any lengthy pursuit should he be unfortunate enough as to have any witnesses to his intended act.

On this last day before Christmas, a full foot of fresh snow had already accumulated on top of the four or five inches which remained from the previous snowfall. The wind had picked up considerably since that morning and, on occasion, its force was so great as to dislodge some of the amassed snow on the roofs' eaves. As larger sections of that denser snow were dislodged from above, the wind would catch the lighter material while breaking the falling mass into smaller pieces. The heavier, compacted snow and ice would come crashing to the ground, while the remaining snow, caught up in the wind, would swirl round and round, creating small localised blizzards. To a child, it would seem like magic; to Kenneth, who rushed through the night with determination, it was an acceptable inconvenience. On several occasions, these snow-filled winds momentarily blinded him, and he was forced to wipe his face and clear his eyes to keep on his bearing.

Walking briskly to help keep warm, Kenneth made his way across the railway line. He had met with few people of interest on the east side of the tracks, and those few he had seen on their own were acquaintances, hardly the people one would pick for a prize. He preferred the western side of the tracks. That part of the town still had some wealth, and very few of those inhabitants knew him by name.

Kenneth made his way through the streets to one of the less frequented shopping areas. Away from the mainstream of that part of the town's economic heart, the harsh reality of the Depression was evident. A number of stores had been boarded up, the businesses therein having failed. Almost every building was in need of repair, yet the more determined shop owners kept their doors open, hoping that better days lay somewhere ahead.

It did not take long for Kenneth to spot a thin lady in a three-quarter-length coat which, even at the distance from which he first saw her, looked like it had seen better days. Yet, she was alone, and for him, that was enough.

He followed a short distance behind, remaining on the opposite side of the street. A few minutes after he began stalking her, the woman walked into a grocery store with its tattered awning hanging askew. That awning was partially rolled up against the lightly snow-covered brick wall, presenting the impression that its latch had failed and was in need of repair. The wind rocked it slightly back and forth, shaking some of the snow off this aged device.

His intended victim remained in the store for only five or six minutes. Then, she emerged with a very small brown paper bag clutched in her hands. Over her left shoulder, Kenneth could see a well-worn thin leather strap attached to a rather grimy white purse.

Keeping slightly behind his intended target, Kenneth began to think.

The storyteller slightly lowered the tone of his voice so as to emphasise the rogue's thoughts.

I'll cut that thin strap through from behind and be off in a second. She'll never even see my face.

Kenneth took a thorough but quick look around before increasing his pace and beginning to cross the narrow street.

Again, the gentleman relating this tale changed the pitch of his voice.

This'll be easy pickings, Kenneth thought as he neared the unsuspecting woman. *I'll be on my way well before she can raise the alarm. There isn't even anyone within calling distance. With this wind, even if anyone is in one of these boarded-up homes, they'll never hear any cry for help.*

Kenneth had almost reached the kerb on the other side and had one hand in his pocket from which he was retrieving a sharp penknife. Suddenly, the wind picked up with such force that his sight was instantly obscured. In that moment of blindness, he missed his step and slipped on the icy surface of the road, falling forward with an unexpected exclamation.

"God's holy trousers!" Kenneth blurted out as he fell forward, his vision still obscured as he hit the ground.

The impact with the kerb was lessened by the amount of snow which had accumulated, but the pain which registered was equivalent to having been hit with a small hammer.

There was no pause in the story whenever the gentleman came to this part of the tale. In fact, his words would flow much faster and in distinct tones.

As Kenneth lifted his aching head off the ground, he found himself lying in the dirt of his old schoolyard. Thomas Burfield, Allan Mizner, and the school's bully, Jack Spratt, surrounded him.

"Get up, you little runt! That punch was just a taste of what you've got coming," Jack yelled. "You know you don't belong here. You're from the wrong side of the tracks and your kind ain't welcome here. Now we catch you hanging around with one of our girls!"

"Kenneth's got a girlfriend! Kenneth's got a girlfriend!" Tommy yelled from the side.

Not wishing to remain in the dirt and have the boys think he was yellow, Kenneth quickly rose to his feet.

Jack was three years older, taller, broad in the shoulders, and had big hands. Those hands were currently curled up to make two big fists which were being thrust at the smaller boy with repeated jabs. Kenneth was able to keep the bigger boy at bay for a time, a dull throb still penetrating in his head. He was smaller, but he was quicker on his feet.

If I could just break and run, Kenneth thought, *I'd be out of this mess, but Tommy and Al are keeping me blocked in.*

Kenneth managed to poke one of his fists through and touch Jack's head before the older boy hit him just above his right eye. The impact stung and he instinctively put one of his hands up to protect the injury. The next second, Jack hit him squarely on the forehead. This was followed by a fake left jab which Kenneth was able to avoid. This evasive manoeuvre, however, was what Jack hoped Kenneth would do. In the next instant, the bully connected with a right which caught him on the jaw. With that impact, he was again sent sprawling to the ground.

"That'll teach ya!" Allan yelled with glee. "You poor folk ain't got no business hangin' round with our girls — no, sir!"

"Kenneth had a girlfriend! Kenneth had a girlfriend!" Tommy shouted in unison with Allan, the verb altered to the past tense to inflict more harm.

Lisi, the girl with whom the other boys had 'caught him' wasn't from the east side of the tracks, but she liked him well enough. As Kenneth raised his head out of the dirt, he looked over in her direction. Lisi had both of her hands covering her face so that they shielded most of the beating from her view. Yet, from where he lay, he could see that she was crying.

Noticing where the fallen boy was looking, Jack turned to the sobbing girl.

"He's not our kind," he said in a gruff voice, "so stop crying like a baby. Best you forget him and be on your way. Now scat!"

Turning his attention back to Kenneth, Jack cautioned, "You'll never be welcome here when I'm around. You don't fit in — none of your kind do, so keep out of our way or I'll do the same, or worse, the next time we meet."

As he lay on the ground, Kenneth could feel the pain from Jack's solid fist connecting with his jaw. There was no use getting back up. Jack would just knock him down again. He was too small and outnumbered to alter the situation. He felt vulnerable, he was ashamed of his helplessness, and reluctantly, he accepted his defeat.

I'd better not look at Jack or he just might kick me while I'm down, Kenneth thought as he lowered his eyes to the ground. *Better leave things as they are; I know when I'm beaten.*

Bringing one hand up to rub the sore point on his bruised face, he slowly looked up and was surprised that the scene of the old schoolyard had vanished. Much to his astonishment, his intended victim, the woman with the tattered three-quarter-length coat, was kneeling by his side. He was back in the snow at the side of the kerb, holding his sore jaw with one hand.

"Mister, are you all right?" the woman asked. "You slipped and almost fell upon me in your hurry — scared me, you did. You hit that kerb hard, mister. Should I go fetch the grocer and get some help?"

Kenneth could not believe the person he was about to rob had remained to offer assistance. Looking over at his free hand, he saw the unopened knife. His glance drew attention to that weapon, and he saw the woman rise and step back a few paces.

As she rose, the woman pointed at the knife.

"W-what's that for?" she stammered. "W-why the knife?"

Straightening himself up, Kenneth replied, "Curse my rotten luck — and pardon the expression, madam — but I ain't no saint, and I'll level with you as you stayed to help. God knows why. I meant to cut your purse strap and run, I did. But someone up there likes you, and He intended that I leave you alone."

Dusting himself off and wishing to leave before the incident drew any unwanted attention, he quickly added, "No harm done, I hope. I'll beg your pardon, madam, and ask your forgiveness. Best be on my way—"

He was about to turn on his heels and vanish into the darkness and the snowstorm when the lady interrupted.

"Rob me? Now that's a laugh. I'm from Cameron Lane and don't even have a penny to my name. If I did, I'd give it to you, I would, as it's Christmas Eve and all."

Stepping forward, the woman opened her bag and showed Kenneth a very small cooked bird.

"See?" she continued. "I've come a long way to this here grocer's. He's a good man, he is — one of a kind. Who else would give me an advance while knowing well enough that he'll likely never be paid in full? Yet, he's got a kind heart, he does, and he still lets me into his store — else why would I be so far from home on a night as cold and miserable as this?"

Having said her piece, the kind-hearted woman closed her bag, turned, and went on her way.

Again, the narrator's voice and tone changed.

How long was I on the ground? What just happened? Kenneth wondered. *I clearly recall that afternoon in the schoolyard, but that was so long ago. If I'm not mistaken, one of my eyes was almost fully closed by the time I got home. My threadbare clothes were dirty, my forehead was cut and bleeding, and I could hardly move my jaw after Jack's well-placed punch.*

Kenneth continued to ponder as he went on his way. *How did I ever forget that feeling? Back then, I felt so unwanted, so alone, and so vulnerable. Sadly, I've changed for the worse over the years.*

Here, it was customary for the gentleman to take a rather lengthy pause. The interruption in the dialogue may have been an attempt to let Kenneth's contemplative thoughts, a moral examination thrust upon him by the fall, sink in. The delay may also have been for the gentleman to adjust his posture and gather his thoughts. Whatever the reason, if sitting, he usually rose and took a few paces away from the fire. If he was standing, he would shake more snow off his heavy coat and take a step or two. At times, he would lift his head and gaze up to the sky, looking at the snowflakes as they fell. On other occasions, I watched as he lazily meandered through the ragged group, looking at no one in particular, but that kind smile evident upon his face. Most of the people present remained where they sat. A few replenished the fire as they added wood, but if anyone spoke during that intermission, those voices were in hushed tones. It was as if no one wished to break the silence the intentional pause had created.

Once the gentleman returned to the side of the fire, a quiet cough was all that was required to indicate he was about to begin anew.

Dazed and with his jaw still in pain from the impact with the kerb, the memory from the past soon faded from Kenneth's thoughts. He felt slightly disappointed with the outcome, but he had more pressing matters at hand.

Kenneth had no idea how long he had lain upon the frozen ground, but he was sure the lady had ample time to have had a good look at his face. She had been kind enough to remain while he was lying injured in the snow, but Kenneth had seen the fear in her eyes when she was aware of the knife.

If she were to encounter a constable in the next few minutes, he had no idea what her reaction might be. Should she blurt out that she had just encountered a man with a weapon, Kenneth was sure the officer would be able to extract a clear and accurate description. Yet, from the look in her face when he came to, and from her addressing him as 'mister', he was certain that she did not know his name, even if she had recognised him from her district. Past experience had taught him that it was best to err on the side of caution, so he made himself scarce the instant they parted.

Darkness had already set in and Kenneth needed to find another mark. There was no use in tempting fate and remaining on the east side of the river while that woman was at large; the chances of being caught were too high. If he meant to score before everyone went home for Christmas, he had to reach the west side of town and quickly.

Making his way to a narrow pedestrian bridge which crossed the river, Kenneth took in the sight. This aged riveted-steel structure had tall cast-iron lanterns set in a row on each side of the bridge's handrail, creating two thin lines of overhead light. The brightness glowing out of panes of glass set into the four sides of the lanterns' slightly tapered heads illuminated each of the falling snowflakes. As they passed through that light, they seemed to sparkle like tiny crystals, a stark contrast against the dark night sky. A child, or any other person who was present, could hardly miss the phenomenal beauty of nature on such a Christmas Eve. In that brief moment, as Kenneth's eyes were caught up in that magical sight of hundreds of flakes flickering past the lantern, he suddenly felt dizzy and had to grab onto the handrail with both hands to keep upright. In that bedazzling instant, his mind flashed back to another time.

Father Martin, the aged pastor of the local church, stood in front of him, a stern look upon his otherwise jovial face. A rim of thin ash-white hair protruded from beneath his black biretta, confirming that he had already lived a long life. The index finger of his right hand wiggled back and forth as the clergy-man spoke.

"You are old enough to know better, young man. The way you just behaved is disrespectful for any adult and you ought to be ashamed. Why, just last week we went over the Ten Commandments in class. I know you were present, as I asked you to recite the fourth. How is it possible you can then act the way you just did toward your mother? I am very disappointed in what I just saw. To be sure you haven't forgotten what was taught, would you be kind enough to repeat that commandment for me once more?"

Kenneth recalled the words and said, "Honour your father and your mother."

He had received a gentle pat on the head. A warm feeling came over him as both his mother and the priest smiled at him.

Taking both of her son's hands firmly in her own, his mother added, "I forgive you for the rude behaviour, and I hope this little speech from Father Martin will stay in that head of yours for a time."

Still clutching Kenneth's hands, she looked up at the priest and said, "God knows I try, father. Yet, he's got a mind of his own even though he's so young. I doubt he'll be good for the rest of the year — but with Christmas coming, who knows? It just might last a few days."

Kenneth could still feel his mother's warm hands as they clutched his. Yet,

as the snowflakes briefly stopped in
their wild descent, the vision vanished,
and he found himself back on the
pedestrian bridge firmly gripping the
iron rail.

What's come over me? he thought. *Why
these flashes into my past? Am I beginning
to lose my mind? I thought I had put my
painful past behind me. What do I have
to gain by recalling my shameful youth and
where I grew up?*

Here, the gentleman who was relating the tale acted
out the next words while he said, "Vigorously shaking
his head, Kenneth straightened himself up, steadied
his feet, and released his iron grasp of the rail."

Lowering the tone of his voice to that which he
used to evoke the rogue's thoughts, the gentleman
continued with his tale.

*Bah, tommyrot. This nostalgia is inter-
fering with what I'm here for,* Kenneth
thought. *It must be the hunger that's
bringing on all of these strange dizzy spells.
I'd better settle down or I'll make a blunder
on account of this delirium that I may well
regret. It could put me behind bars.*

Never looking back, Kenneth
crossed the bridge over to the west

bank. Before he entered the core of the business section, Kenneth came upon the rather wide promenade which followed the river's edge. For the use of the occasional private carriage, a second path made of a different type of cobblestone ran parallel to the pedestrian walkway. That part of the walkway had an imprint of a single track visible in the snow, indicating that it had recently been used.

The entire promenade had been built sometime after the First World War, but it was reminiscent of the Victorian age. Ornate lampposts rose at appropriate intervals from a snow-covered metal railing which skirted the edge of the river. Next to the impressive barrier, benches on which a person could idle their time or rest, when the seats weren't covered in snow, were conveniently placed at regular intervals marked by a walking distance of no more than one hundred feet. To the side of the paved path, another wide expanse of soft snow lay on the ground, covering a green belt which consisted of mown grass in the warmer months.

Between this park-like setting and the town, a dense band of evergreen trees had been planted in a concerted effort to keep the noise of the city from penetrating the serenity of the area. The pedestrian footpath had been designed so that there was no direct access to the town's core from where the bridge ended. One had to follow the promenade for some distance before coming upon one of the broad clearings which provided access to the business district.

As Kenneth walked toward one of those exits, he came upon a grove of tall fir trees which had been densely planted near the edge of the paved path. The proximity of these trees partially obscured the walkway as it followed a bend in the river. The branches of each tree were distinctly bent under the weight of the freshly fallen snow. As Kenneth neared this grove, the snow at times shifted with the wind, causing a branch to discharge some of its burden of snow. A small cascade of flakes would trickle down to a lower branch. As the snow from above landed upon a particular limb, the lower offshoot was also put off balance, releasing some of its snowpack. This small avalanche flowed from one branch onto the next, tipping each limb over on its way to the ground. The wind picked up some of the lighter material and sent it flying through the air, adding to the amount of snow already airborne. That combination of wind and snow quite obscured visibility as Kenneth brusquely walked along the promenade.

If I'm not careful, he thought, *I might miss my step and end up in the deeper, softer snow which covers the carriage path or grass.*

As he had already fallen once that evening, Kenneth slowed his pace.

Making his way around the group of tall evergreens, Kenneth could not believe what lay ahead.

God's holy trousers! My fortune has just changed for the better, he thought.

In a small clearing just ahead, fully blocked from all sides except for the river, a smartly matched pair of horses stood quite still, their hindquarters toward him. Off to the side and in the deeper snow lay an overturned curricle. Had this coach been pulled by a single steed, Kenneth might have called it a chaise. It was most unusual to have such a small vehicle pulled by a team of horses, but it meant that the owner likely had money. Looking just to the right of the overturned vehicle, he could see the back of a smartly dressed gentleman in a thick, dark winter coat lying with his limbs stretched out and face-down in the snow.

In his haste, Kenneth thought, *the owner likely pushed the horses faster than the weather permitted. The driver's visibility, hampered by the falling snow, was perhaps questionable and he made an error. One of the large, thin wooden wheels must have left the cobblestone path and resulted in a sudden imbalance of the vehicle – the blessing of which is before me.*

Just a short distance from where the driver lay in a most ungraceful posture, a number of brightly wrapped packages lay scattered around the overturned coach. Quickening his pace, Kenneth wished to take advantage of the situation before the owner came to his wits.

The gentleman spinning this Christmas yarn quickened the rate of his speech to help exemplify Kenneth's nefarious motions.

Nearing the site of the accident, Kenneth quickly scanned the entire area to assess the situation. Not more than a few feet from the driver, a bulky black *porte-monnaie* protruded from the snow. It lay where it had fallen, directly beneath one of the tall evergreens in the hollow of the snow these trees make. In deep mountain snow, these pits often become a hazard to an unwary skier.

Even better luck, I'd say, Kenneth thought as he raced over to where the wallet was poking out of the snow. *In a second, it'll be mine and no one will be the wiser. With all this snow about, it's not likely anyone would ever find it until spring. With the condition the fellow's in, it's not likely he'd even notice it's missing. If he does, I just might help him look for it. Who knows? He's likely to have a leather satchel with a few loose coins; most gents of his sort do. In his plight, he might just be inclined to give me a penny or two for the extra effort. Not that it'll be found, mind you.* A sly expression began to form on Kenneth's face.

Stopping a foot from where the wallet lay, he bent down and snatched the sizeable purse up with his left hand. In that moment, the winter wind howled through the mass of branches, and a powerful gust blew up from the river, causing the snow to fly wildly about. For an instant, the larger snow-laden braches swayed in that blast of wind. The next moment, the heavy built-up snow broke free from above, striking the branches below. The newly loosened snow and ice cascaded down with such energy and mass that Kenneth was almost instantly knocked down by its weight. In an involuntary act of self-preservation and survival, he placed his free right hand before his face to shield against any impact, while lifting his left hand up into the air. It was an action of pure instinct, yet it prevented him from losing the man's wallet.

"Blast the bleeding snow," Kenneth muttered more to himself than to anyone else. "Been a bloody nuisance this whole night, it has."

Then, as his head came out from under the snow, he was astounded at what he beheld.

While another narrator might revel in the drama of the situation and pause for effect, the gentleman telling the story continued without even stopping to take a short breath.

Kenneth's frail mother was standing before him, waving a finger much as Father Martin had in the vision he had seen on the bridge. He was a year or two older, and his mother was quite angry about what he held in his hands. Reaching out with aged hands that were not customarily that quick, she snatched a black wallet out of his hands before he could react.

"No telling where you got it, yet there's no use aggravating the situation, so I'll believe what you said, that you just found it," his mother said in the tone of voice she used whenever she was angry with him. "Now, Kenneth, there's no use arguing with me. You know full well you cannot keep it. It's simply not the Christian thing to do."

Briefly looking up to the heavens, she continued with a groan, "God, please help me in teaching my boy the difference between what's right and wrong."

Opening the wallet, she began to thumb through the items inside while

making a frown and saying, "Oh."
Discovering some item which must
have identified the wallet, her face
brightened and she followed with
"Ah!"

Turning to face her son, his mother
removed a single paper therein and
said, "Seems like it belongs to Mr
Grumbolt, and you, *sir* — you and I
are going to take it to him this very
minute!"

Mr Grumbolt was a local banker,
one of the more unpleasant ones.
He had turned Kenneth's father
down for a loan on more than one
occasion. The nights which followed
those unsuccessful meetings had not
been pleasant. Kenneth would have
preferred not to have to go along to
visit Mr Grumbolt, but that was not
an option.

With those heated words spoken
and, hopefully, still lingering in her
son's head, his mother snatched one of
her better bonnets from the coatrack
and took off her soiled apron. Putting
on the only coat she owned, she pulled
a pair of tattered woollen gloves from
its pockets and took Kenneth firmly by

one hand. Without another word, she marched him out of that old rooming house and onto the street.

Kenneth's family lived in an older set of soot-blackened brick row houses just west of Cameron Lane. As a youth, he had often been told that they were a bit better off than their neighbours to the east, yet he liked the kids he met from there as much as any other child he knew. While he was young, and especially while his mother was still alive, he never sensed that he did not live a normal life. Everyone around had the same needs; and, as a child under the age of nine, poverty is not something about which one is overly concerned. Other than the taunting at school, he had everything a child needed. His mother took care of him, and as long as his father was sober, he did as well as any other boy who lived in the area. In fact, many kids only had a mother who could look after them, as their fathers had often left before or shortly after they were born.

To reach Mr Grumbolt's home, they had to cross the railway tracks and the east side of the town. Then, they had to walk over the narrow pedestrian bridge to the west side of the river. From there, they had to make their way through the business section and into the more affluent part of town.

At this point in the story, the gentleman would briefly rise and again shake off any accumulated snow from his hair and coat. At times, one could hear him sigh before he would settle down and continue.

Kenneth knew his mother's resolve, and he didn't need Father Martin's prodding; he knew perfectly well that one should not steal nor covet a neighbour's goods. In his mother's eye, he had likely broken at least one of these ancient, unalterable rules by which any God-fearing Christian should live. The route they had to follow, however, was far too long for Kenneth to just quietly hang onto his mother's firm grasp. Kenneth whined and moaned to show his distaste, but he generally kept from saying any understandable words. Those would just result in a stern reprimand and a delay of the journey. In his mind, this trek was a form of torture, a punishment a child must simply endure.

Eventually, the more imposing mansions which the well-to-do call their homes appeared. Tall stone columns of various sizes and shapes held roofs of diverse architectural styles, each covering an impressive set of steps. All the homes had massive front doors, some sporting two of a similar design. Wrought-iron gates barred the entrances to the walkways of several of the more palatial estates. Most had a second entrance which had been built to accommodate a horse and a carriage; all were at least two storeys high and in good repair. Chimneys and gables adorned the roof of each building, presenting a pleasing picture to the young boy. Yet, his mother did not stop to admire the impressive buildings. She was on a mission; only one house interested her in the slightest and that was the three-storey home in which Mr Grumbolt lived.

Kenneth's mother did not hesitate in opening the black wrought-iron gate which led to the property. At the bottom of the landing, his mother stopped. Turning to the boy, she handed the sizeable *porte-monneaie* back.

"Now, young man," his mother said, "you and I are going up these stairs, and we are going to return this wallet to its proper owner. Is that understood?" Not waiting for an answer, she continued, "We may be poor, but we have our pride — I have my Christian morals and I want *you to learn from this.*" The last words were spoken with some intensity.

Holding onto Kenneth's right hand, she pulled her somewhat reluctant son up behind her. Despite her age, she climbed those stone steps as if the flight had never existed, Kenneth moaning and groaning with each new tier. When she was satisfied that Kenneth stood by her side and was somewhat presentable, his mother pulled rather dramatically upon the bell rope.

Kenneth could hear the peal of that lonely bell and anticipated the irate and grumpy demeanour of the banker who was being summoned by its knell. He was certain that it was the harbinger of an impending and foreboding doom.

"As I have mentioned in telling you this Christmas story," the gentleman relating the tale would say, "Mr Grumbolt was known as a rather hard-hearted banker. I wish to make it clear that Kenneth knew that 'his kind' were not the sort of folk to which one loaned money. In fact, Mr Grumbolt followed the age-old practice of loaning money only if the bank knew that the individual in question was in a position where they could pay it back or, if in default, had equity which his bank could seize."

As Kenneth and his mother waited for the door to open, he had time to reflect. *If it had been up to me, I would have jumped at the chance to get revenge by keeping the money. Yet, Mum's views on revenge reflect those of the Bible,*

"Vengeance is mine, sayeth the Lord," and they are not to be questioned.

A tall, thin, stoic-looking butler in a black tuxedo opened the door.

"May I help you, madam?" he said without any emotion evident in those memorable words.

"We've come to see Mr Grumbolt, sir," was Kenneth's mother's simple reply.

"Mr Grumbolt has no appointments scheduled today, madam," the butler replied. "I have been instructed that he is not available to anyone today, I'm sorry to—"

Kenneth's mother cut him off. "We have Mr Grumbolt's wallet. I'm sure he will see us," she persisted.

Without asking them to enter and providing some brief shelter from the cold, the butler replied, "One moment, please."

He shut the door.

Within two or three minutes, a duration of time wherein Kenneth tried to pull his hand out from under his mother's tight grip, the door was opened once more. The same well-dressed employee appeared.

"Madam," he said, looking down at them, "Mr Grumbolt has instructed me to look the article over, and if it is his missing wallet, I am to accept it on his behalf. The master is clear in his wish not to receive anyone without an—"

Again Kenneth's mother interrupted the butler. "No, sir! My son found it, and he will only give it to the owner directly. It's to be a lesson to my son as to what's right and what is wrong — giving the wallet to you and not Mr Grumbolt will not have the same effect, and that is simply wrong. You may go and tell your employer that the wallet is here at his doorstep. I will only permit my son to give it to him and to him alone."

Her voice had a tone of assurance Kenneth had never heard her use before. It had, however, the desired effect, and the butler shut the door once again.

In short order, the butler opened the massive door and Mr Grumbolt was at his side. The banker, a person Kenneth had never met, appeared to be in his late fifties, was evidently overweight, and was smoking an ornate curved pipe. He sported a full head of greying hair parted on the left side, but his face had a creased frown which clearly displayed the displeasure he must have felt at having to deal with the issue personally. As he looked down at the boy holding his wallet, his frown added a fold or two and his lip curled upward under his nose, turning the look into a more menacing glare.

"Humph!" was the first word which came from his mouth. Then, bending down to almost Kenneth's level, he continued, "Likely as not, you were one of the scrawny street urchins at the market the other day. That's the precise day on which I first noticed the item in your hand was missing."

Before the boy could reply, Mr Grumbolt crouched down and snatched his leather *porte-monnaie* from Kenneth's trembling, outstretched hand.

Mr Grumbolt took the time to stand up to his full height and Kenneth, watching the feet wobble under the tension applied, wondered if the banker's legs would even be able to lift all of that mass. Yet, without the help of the butler, the old man managed to rise to his feet.

Keeping his menacing eye on the poor boy, he added, "Be glad it's almost Christmas and that I don't call on the constabulary and have you both put into irons." Turning toward the mother, Mr Grumbolt pointed an accusing finger in her direction before he went on with his curt oration. "You, madam, for not keeping a better eye on your son — but that's forgiven by your bringing the boy around to my home — a guilty conscience if you ask me. And you . . ." Here, his gaze again took in the boy. The expression on Mr Grumbolt's face had turned as black as any Kenneth had ever seen. "And you, young scallywag, for being the likely pickpocket in the first place."

With those harsh words, he turned his back upon the pair, leaving his butler to continue.

"You heard the master. Now be off with you both!" he barked.

Then, rather unceremoniously, he shut the great door with an audible bang.

Kenneth would never forget that moment of humiliation and shame. The noise of the door closing on their faces had brought him and his mother to the attention of several of the people close by. At first, these more affluent individuals raised their eyebrows slightly, portraying an inquisitive look. Once they noticed the tattered clothing, those faces contorted with deep lines and downturned lips, expressing looks of scorn and contempt.

Kenneth had been wrong in thinking the money he found could be kept. His mother had been clear on that matter. His mother even had the resolve to make him personally hand his discovery back to Mr Grumbolt. That man, however, had not shown an ounce of appreciation. Instead of thanking them, Mr Grumbolt had accused Kenneth of lying and had gone so far as to insinuate that both he and his mother were somehow at fault, that they could have been punished, regardless of guilt.

Kenneth had learned a lesson that day. Money seemed to hold immense power. A good position and being well off were of a higher value than truth. Showing a person of a perceived lower class the door after a false accusation, without even permitting the injured party to say their piece, seemed to absolve the wealthy of any further obligations. It was far from the lesson his mother had intended.

At this point, the narrator would again rise and briefly rub his hands together. Looking over the spellbound group, he would rest his vocal cords for a few moments before he would continue.

Kenneth had begun his nefarious road to what he had become, to what drove him out onto the street that Christmas Eve, shortly after his beating at school. His mother had already passed away and that memorable evening he'd had to mend his torn clothes with his own hands.

The following year, shortly after his older brother left home, he dropped out of school and met up with a few other youths in similar situations. For a time, to satisfy the pangs of hunger, he had been like the street urchins of Mr Grumbolt's accusation. Perhaps those unjust words had been a premonition of what lay ahead. In time, he fell in with a Fagin type, who was wily enough to keep him from prison and honed Kenneth's skill as a pickpocket. Yet, the memory of Mr Grumbolt's unjust actions made him feel distaste at having to hand wallets over to anyone, including his newfound teacher. As a result, the Fagin and Kenneth soon had a quarrel, and he broke out on his own, now confident that the old thief had nothing further to offer.

Kenneth could still feel Mr Grumbolt tearing that wallet out of his left hand. In fact, he could still see his mother as she pulled him along.

Incredible, Kenneth had thought as they'd crossed over the iron bridge and made their way over to the east side of the river. *Why are people so rude? Why do they dislike us and distrust us just because we're poor?*

All these strange feelings differ from Mother's view. What's to become of me? he contemplated.

As those perplexing thoughts faded, so too did the image of Kenneth's mother as she dragged him homeward by his left hand. Yet, the feeling of her pulling him along remained as strong as ever.

In the next instant, he found his head emerging from the snow which had buried him. Looking over his left shoulder, he could see that his left hand was still firmly gripping the sizeable black wallet and a man's hand was gripping the other end.

This is just plain crazy! Kenneth thought. *I can't be back at Mr Grumbolt's door. A moment ago, I imagined Mother was pulling me along. Have I gone mad?*

Looking up and away from the wallet in his left hand, Kenneth saw that the person presently applying that force was not Mr Grumbolt. Another person's hand was attached to the other end of that wallet and it had pulled him out of the snowpack in which he had been buried. This hand belonged to the gentleman who had been thrown from his carriage.

"Good God, man, are you all right?" a good-humoured voice called out. "So very kind of you to have come to my aid, and I see that you have found my wallet. With all this deep snow about, it is most fortunate that you chanced upon my way and my purse. Without your quick actions and with the snow which fell from these trees burying everything in sight, I doubt I would ever have found it on my own."

At a slight disadvantage from what had just taken place and his head in a whirl, Kenneth found himself voluntarily passing the *porte-monnaie* back to the smiling gentleman.

"Help me put the wagon upright, sir," the stranger said, his smile broadening as he spoke, "and I'll gladly give you a fiver for your kind assistance."

A *fiver!* Kenneth's thoughts raced wildly. *Five pounds sterling! Five pounds earned, at that!*

Kenneth could hardly believe his ears. He had no steady income. England had an official overall unemployment rate of fifteen percent in 1932, likely much higher in the cities. Those people he knew who did have a job were lucky to get just over a pound for a fifty-hour working week.

That amount of money was well over a month's wages for many of the non-unionised working people he knew.

Kenneth had that curricle upright in a moment and helped pick up all of the fallen packages without the gentleman having to say another word. It was, after all, the right thing to do.

With all of the goods safely back in the carriage, the gentleman turned and looked Kenneth over with a keen eye. Satisfied by what he saw and with a kind smile upon his rosy face, he pulled out the black wallet. Opening that money satchel, he selected a crisp new five-pound note and handed it to Kenneth.

"A promise is a promise," the gentleman said in an earnest but soft voice. "I do thank you for all you have done. Some higher being must have intervened, because — and I do beg your pardon, as I mean no offence for saying it — by the appearance of your attire, I doubt you chance upon this part of the river very often. Yet, your timing was impeccable, and you were able to retrieve my wallet before the snow from that tree buried it. God bless you, sir!"

Shaking Kenneth's hand vigorously, he added, "A very, and I repeat sir, a very Merry Christmas to you!"

Prior to closing his wallet, the gentleman pulled out a neatly printed business card and passed that calling card to Kenneth in addition to the money.

"Please do look me up if ever there is anything I could do for you. One really never knows when someone can use a little help. Today's a good example and" The gentleman broke off, pausing long enough to again shake Kenneth's hand. "And a Merry Christmas to you, kind sir."

Stepping into his open ride, the man grasped the reins and had his horses move off.

It had been a long time since anyone had said kinder words to Kenneth than those which the gentleman had just spoken. They were sincere and heartfelt syllables; they meant a lot to him. For some reason which he was not able to quantify, a warm, almost unfamiliar feeling rose in his heart. He no longer felt the cold nipping at his exposed skin. The snow was still falling and the wind was still blowing, possibly even harder than before, but as he shook the snow off his threadbare dark-blue peacoat, he no longer felt the winter's chill.

With five pounds sterling in his pocket, there was no further reason to continue working that night. If he hurried back over the river, he could easily reach Mahony's Irish Pub before it closed for the night. That establishment would provide shelter from the elements and, if he chose to eat, a warm meal. However, the most urgent draw to that public house was the lure of a good pint of ale. Mahony's welcomed riffraff, providing they came in the door with cash, and Kenneth had more than enough of that on hand. If he were to watch his spending, those five pounds could

last him until the end of January, but
Kenneth knew himself well enough
not to contemplate such prudence.

Lowering the pitch of his voice to signify the
miscreant's thoughts, the gentleman relating the tale
continued.

*I'll drink myself into oblivion, most likely
as not,* Kenneth thought as a broad
smile began crossing his face. *When
I've got money, I'm not known to be a
tightwad, no sir! I'm not like some of those
other blokes I've known.*

Returning to his usual tone of voice, the storyteller
continued.

In fact, there were few bars on the
poor side of town wherein Kenneth
had not bought a round or two over
the years. Mind you, there was a
bit of a payback contained in those
benevolent, free-spending times, but
that was of little concern on that
particular Christmas Eve.
Yes, in those days, when Kenneth was
inebriated, and he meant to be before
that night was over, he was everyone's
best friend. Those friendships usually

lasted only until his funds ran dry and the owner threw him out of the establishment. For the moment, he was rich, and as was his custom, he lived for the moment.

It took less than five minutes to reach the riveted-iron bridge and begin his return crossing. Kenneth had not a care in the world and thought only of the beer he was about to enjoy.

I'm sure I'll fit in a bit of food before the night is over, Kenneth thought, with an inner warmth building within his tattered coat. *Yes, tonight will be a most memorable Christmas Eve indeed!*

After the gentleman relating this story had spoken the word 'indeed!', he would briefly scan the faces of all those who had gathered to listen. A warm smile lit his slightly weathered face, the cap of fresh snow on his head giving him a most jovial appearance. Satisfied with the attentive audience, he would continue.

The lanterns still burned brightly on the bridge, their flickering attuned to the force of the passing wind. Snow still fell and passed through the glow of each light, causing those flakes to

momentarily take on another hue.
Briefly, they sparkled in the amber
radiance of the lamp overhead.
Once they were out of that artificial
illumination, they again took on
their original white, adding to the
blanket of snow as they landed upon
a handrail or the footpath. Yet, as
Kenneth crossed, he neither noticed
that natural beauty nor recalled the
memories of Father Martin or Mr
Grumbolt. Those strange images from
his past were no longer in the forefront
of his mind. All he could think of was
the first pint of thirst-quenching beer
and the camaraderie he would share
with the patrons which he would meet
at Mahony's.

Yes, Kenneth thought, *before that
public house closes, it will be a most
enjoyable Christmas Eve, indeed.*

Once he reached the far side of the
river, lampposts and their brilliant
glow became less frequent. It was as if
society did not wish to see the squalor
and filth often present in the less
affluent parts of the town. Kenneth,
however, was one who cherished
darkness and couldn't care less if there

were any lampposts at all. Darkness
increased the success within his chosen
profession, his nefarious trade, and he
welcomed it with an open heart.

As he entered a rather dark, narrow
alley, only a few blocks away from
Mahony's, the wind increased and
blew through that slender passage with
a fury. The snow, again falling much
more intensely, flew wildly about,
almost blinding him. A prudent man
would have halted to clear his eyes, or
at least slowed his pace, but Kenneth
was not inclined to ponder the safety
of that particular situation. When he
had a mission, it was his custom to
act blindly and on instinct. Thus, he
pressed on without altering his stride.

Once or twice, he put his hand out
to touch the side of one of the high
walls which rose on both sides of the
narrow lane. Very little snow had
actually landed within its confines, yet
the path underfoot was as white as the
snow-filled air. After a short distance,
the alley opened up onto a wider road
and the Irish pub would have been
visible if not for the winter storm.

Kenneth moved through the snowstorm as silently as a cat. Through

the thin, worn soles of his shoes,
he could feel the missing flagstones
and the uneven paving stones, some
more raised than others. Had the
storm abated and had it been a clear
winter night, he might have seen the
difference in height between the raised
stone footpath to his left and the lower
part which comprised the roadway.
With more than a foot of fresh snow
covering the ground, the whirling
wind was creating small snowdrifts
and no such contrast was visible that
night.

Suddenly, he felt his foot touch the
edge of a particularly sharp, protruding
cobblestone and that appendage
slipped. Once more, he felt himself
falling forward. Once again, he instinctively threw his hands forward, but
he must have misjudged the trajectory
of that fall.

The left side of his head stung on
impact.

"Gad!" he unintentionally blurted
out. "That bloody well hurt!"

He rolled away from the kerb and
momentarily lay face-down at the side
of the road. For several seconds, he let
the coolness of the deep snow soothe

the injured area. Then, he slowly began to rise from where he had fallen.

As Kenneth raised himself up and out of the snow, he could easily see light streaming out of the windows of Mahony's. The long strands of silver, red, and green tinsel, however, were hanging stock-still and the air was no longer filled with the swirling snow. Amazingly, it was now a crisp, clear winter night.

Here, the storyteller always took another short break, often rising and walking a few strides before resuming his strange Christmas tale. In all the years I heard this gentleman tell his story, there was always a warm smile which crossed his pleasant face as he paced during this interlude.

Raised voices could be heard issuing from behind the closed door of Mahony's. The volume of this din increased as he looked in the bar's direction. For some reason, Kenneth remained where he stood, next to a lamppost, taking in the scene and the events as they unfolded.

The door to Mahony's suddenly opened and the oldest of the owner's sons held wide that seasonally decorated portal. Emerging from behind Mahony's son was a raggedly dressed man who was being pushed through the doorway by the bar's owner. The proprietor held the besotted man firmly by the shirt collar and trousers and appeared to be ejecting this particular customer from his premises.

To Kenneth's astonishment, the individual being thrown out of Mahony's was none other than his own father.

Without stopping, the storyteller immediately altered the tone of his voice to suggest the rogue's thoughts.

Impossible — that can't be! My father's long dead, Kenneth thought.

As he watched this scene unfold, he became aware that this was another event from years gone by. His mother was still alive — she died very early the following year — and his brother was by his side.

As the two young boys watched their father being manhandled and tossed into the street, the pub's owner barked out, "On Christmas Eve, sir! Of all the nights of the year — not a coin in your pocket! You should be ashamed to call yourself a man. What will your family eat this night? What grief will you bring home to your good wife? Be gone and may God find a cure for you and your like!"

With those stinging words said, the owner and his son turned their backs upon Kenneth's father. Walking back into the bar, they let the door close with an audible bang.

With the door to the pub closed, Kenneth and his brother watched as their father remained sprawled in the snow. After a few moments of inactivity, the drunken man rose and turned toward the door behind which the elder Mahony son was looking through the door's window.

"Bah!" the man yelled. "I've been thrown out of worse places by better men than you! Your kind all think you're of a higher breed." Then, raising one hand and shaking his fist in defiance, he added, "Just watch if I ever set foot in your foul-smelling tavern when I do have a few coins to my name. You'll see me pass you by — that's what you'll see — and, and you think you've tarnished my good name by this! You're foolin' no man, no sir! There's no shame in being poor and takin' advantage of those who have so much!"

Without bothering to wipe either grime or snow from his clothes, their dishevelled father turned and began to stagger in their direction. As he slowly moved forward, he began to weep.

That was the only time Kenneth had ever heard their father cry in public. Within the community in which they lived, he had never before shown fear or softness. Outside the confines of their small home, he was the man of the house; at home, when the terrible fights over his drunken condition and lack of money were finally over, his father often broke down and cried, asking their mother for pity and forgiveness.

That night had been different. As their father neared, Kenneth could clearly hear his sobs and the pain-filled words.

"God, why me?" he whined. "Why now? Why on this holy night? What have I done? Oh God, what will become of my family? Why have I failed my dear wife? I know the path which lies before me, but why — on this night of all nights — why place this burden on me? On them? Why am I so weak? Why?"

Their father passed and his words became less distinct as he walked away. The sobs, however, could still be heard coming from the penniless and broken man.

These pitiful lamentations were momentarily joined by a new sound which came from the opposite direction. Turning toward Mahony's, Kenneth could hear the distant jingle of a single bell, a bell likely attached to a horse-drawn sleigh. He also became aware that he was alone on the street, his brother no longer at his side.

The knell of the bell became louder and a dull, vague shape resembling a horse pulling a sleigh became visible in the distance, its oil lamps barely cutting through the dark night.

As it neared, it became a much clearer image and reminded him of a sleigh he had seen once before.

Odd, Kenneth thought. *Very odd – few people in these parts have coin enough to eat, let alone hire a covered sleigh.*

It did not stop at the tavern. As it advanced, Kenneth leaned forward to get a view of who might be using this transport. To his astonishment, he noted that this sleigh was carrying a coffin – the coffin of his mother. In that astounding moment, he recognised the sleigh for what it was, and a cold shiver ran up his spine.

He suddenly felt dizzy. He had to hold onto the lamppost to keep from falling over.

As the rapidly disappearing sleigh moved into the distance, Kenneth recovered his balance. He noted that the snow had again begun to fall. Soon the night, the snow, and the distance which separated them obliterated any image of that bizarre sleigh. In that same time frame, Kenneth found that he was a man once more and had five pounds in his pocket. Mahony's lay in the distance, but with the amount of snow which was coming down, he could barely make out its shape.

This was another point in the tale where the gentleman would take a pause. By this time, the fire would need to be stoked. It was common for a few of the listeners to rise and add more wood. After a minute or two, a brighter flame would become visible. Satisfied with their work, those who had risen would return to their places of relative comfort. With a twinkle in his eyes, the narrator would continue with this strange Christmas story.

The lights from inside Mahony's were all aglow. The tinsel had changed shape from what had been there when his father had been evicted but sparkled just as brightly as before. A large natural wreath, partially covered in snow, adorned the door. Its size and shape blocked most of the pane which served as the lone window to

that portal. Christmas carols could
be heard from within, no two voices
in tune. The volume, however, spoke
of the enthusiasm with which these
songs were being sung.

For some reason which he could
not quantify, Kenneth stopped at
the threshold just before entering
the tavern. He looked down at the
well-worn long brass door handle. Its
polished surface offered evidence as
to where many a hand had gripped
its welcoming surface. It served its
purpose well.

Leaning forward, he grasped the
handle with an outstretched arm. In
that instant, the memory of his father's
eviction through that door returned
once again.

Altering his voice to a slightly lower pitch, the storyteller continued.

Mother – God rest her soul, Kenneth
recalled, *had sent my brother and me to
the tavern an hour or so before. We had
been charged with the almost impossible
task of reasoning with Father before he
squandered all of his earnings.*
*Father was well liquored up by the
time we arrived, and he sent us packing,*

Kenneth thought. *I recall that he cuffed both of us soundly behind the ears for our impertinence. Yes, that's the word he used that memorable night, 'impertinence'.*

Yes, Kenneth continued to reason, *with the help of one of Mahony's younger sons, the two of us were shown this very door. Once outside on that clear, cold winter night, we huddled in a nearby alcove partly sheltered from the light wind. There, with my brother's arm tucking me close to his side, we waited for more than an hour. Later, we watched as Father was pushed through this same door.*

Their arrival at home was anything but festive. The screaming and the fight which ensued had been tumultuous. The meal served on that Christmas Eve had been made of one scrawny goose. It was to be their last as a family; his mother died three weeks later.

Again, the tone of voice of the speaker was altered to represent Kenneth's thoughts.

It must have been about the same size as the small bird being carried by the woman I tried to rob, Kenneth suddenly thought. *My God! That night when*

Father was shown the door at Mahony's, I had promised Mother never to follow in his footsteps. How could I have forgotten that vow? Why have I not held to my oath?

For just a moment longer, Kenneth envisioned the meagre feast his mother had served on that Christmas Eve so very long ago. Then, as his thoughts turned to the present, he could see the woman he had tried to rob.

In her condition, she's likely still on her way to Cameron Lane, Kenneth thought. *I might still be able to find her.*

The moment that thought formed, he turned his back on the public house and the temporary relief it promised. Without any regard for his safety, Kenneth ran from that establishment as fast as the snow and his ageing legs would permit.

Once more, wood was added to the fire and a short intermission in the Christmas story took place. With the snow falling, as it usually was, that square was an odd but most pleasant scene to behold. Few outsiders would expect to see such a gathering in that dilapidated part of the town. Yet, it happened just the same, and when everyone had returned to their places, the speaker continued.

Cameron Lane, if one knows the narrow, darker side of the town, is only a stone's throw from the Irish pub.

On a night like this, Kenneth reasoned, *the woman I tried to rob would hardly use the more dangerous but shorter routes in this part of town. If I'm quick about it, I might still be able to find her before she reaches her destination.*

Being well acquainted with the narrow and forlorn parts of the eastern side of the river — useful knowledge when being pursued by either the public or the constabulary — Kenneth made short work of reaching Cameron Lane. He arrived just as the raggedly dressed woman carrying a small wrapped bundle came into view. She was at the entrance to the small alley from which Kenneth had just emerged. His sudden appearance startled her.

Rushing forth with renewed vigour, he must have been a sorry sight to behold on such a stormy winter night. Unkempt and dishevelled from the falls to the ground, he burst onto the street almost as if he had come out of nowhere. The poor woman, having already seen this man with a knife in his hand, noted that he was coming straight toward her. Instantly, she turned and ran. In her terror, she dropped the small package and fled, screaming as she went.

"Help! Help!" she screamed in a high-pitched voice. "Oh God, someone please help me!"

Kenneth, without missing a step, bent down and snatched the bundle from the snow wherein it lay. Then, increasing his pace, he called out as gently as he could.

"Madam, madam! Please forgive me for coming upon you so suddenly. I mean you no harm this time. Heaven forbid — Heaven be praised!"

Seeing that these words had little effect, he slowed his pace and called out in heartfelt tones, "I've learned my lesson. I've learned a lesson or two this night and I mean to change my ways. Please stop. I've been blessed with honest work. Trivial work, really, but I've been paid a king's ransom for it, I have. Please stop. I just want to pass this wonderful gift on to you."

With the poor woman still running and screaming at the top of her lungs, Kenneth stopped his pursuit.

"Look!" he shouted. "Look, I've stopped chasing you and I've even picked up your goose. If you don't stop, it'll be cold before you ever get to take it home."

In frustration, he held out his hands in a gesture of peace.

As those last words struck home, the woman stopped screaming. With Kenneth standing stock-still, no further heavy footsteps could be heard in her wake; the poor woman slowed her pace. When she believed that a sufficient distance separated them, she stopped altogether. Slowly, she turned and looked upon the man who had appeared out of nowhere and had been running after her.

A few of the adjoining homes had lights appear in the windows. Several curious faces could be seen as those inside took a look at what was occurring outside. Yet, no one actually opened a door; Cameron Lane was a place where people minded their own business. It seemed safer that way.

At this point in the story, the gentleman often took his last pause. Then, with a final look upon the hushed crowd, the twinkle in his eyes would become more evident, and he would continue with his story.

With the poor woman looking on from a distance, Kenneth proudly held up her discarded package and smiled. It was the first time in at least a decade that he could recall a time when he had sincerely smiled. Yet, on that particular Christmas Eve, Kenneth smiled all the same.

"Madam, it's true — I mean you no harm," Kenneth could hear himself say. "Today, I've somehow been blessed with recalling moments in my past, moments long forgotten, but their meaning has taught me much. It began when I lay in the snow by the grocer's shop at your feet. Those forgotten moments were repeated a few times since and through it all, I've been rewarded — with more than I could have imagined. I want to change and . . ."

Here, Kenneth paused, praying that he'd find the correct words to convey what he felt in his heart. "And I would like to share that wonder, that blessing with you."

Those words had the effect Kenneth had hoped. The poor frightened creature's face, barely discernible in the distance, calmed and she began to cautiously approach. As she neared, she came into the light which issued from under the lone streetlamp upon that road, at the entrance to Cameron Lane. It was the first time in a long while that Kenneth had taken a close look at anyone's face. In his line of work, the faces of others were best forgotten.

To his amazement, Kenneth saw that this poor woman was not some old hag, but looked to be a lady just past her prime. Although the lines of time and her hard existence were etched upon her weathered face, she still held a certain beauty. In fact, as she came closer and he could see that face more clearly, Kenneth found her to be quite pretty.

In that moment of mutual inspection, she also broke out into a weak smile and took the small package from his outstretched hand.

Still smiling, he doffed his snow-covered cap and simply said, "Good evening, madam. My name is Kenneth, Kenneth Chadwick."

Without permitting him to continue, the woman replied in a soft voice, "I'm called Monica, Monica Walker, and I'm glad to meet you on better terms."

For a moment, the two were silent. Searching for answers, their eyes unmasked the gruff, weathered exterior each portrayed in a casual glance. Satisfied by what she saw, Monica was the first to speak.

"Would you like to join me for dinner? It's not much and probably not too warm, but I'd like to share what I have with you."

That night, in the tiny little home wherein Monica lived, Kenneth had a Christmas feast which he has never forgotten.

Within days of that Christmas Eve, Kenneth called upon the man who had presented him with the business card. That kind fellow owned a shipyard and required an apprentice shipwright, a position Kenneth readily accepted. Learning from his fellow workers, he became proficient in the skills of the trade.

Within a year, Monica and Kenneth were married. Shortly thereafter, that communion was blessed by the birth of a son, followed by the arrival of three daughters.

Kenneth never forgot that strange Christmas. Indeed, he continued to work hard and within seven years, he became a journeyman. He never fell back or returned to his old ways; he matured and became a foreman within the firm. By the time his third daughter was old enough to enter school, Kenneth had become superintendent of the firm.

Monica and Kenneth taught their children to understand difficult times and to accept people at face value. They showed them how to look for positive traits in each individual. By example, they taught them to offer help but only if guidance or assistance was needed. They also never forgot to share their newfound wealth.

Kenneth still smiles to this day. Each and every Christmas, until the old grocer died in the poorer part of that town, he crossed over that iron bridge with Monica and their family, handing out large birds to each and every person on the grocer's list of those who could not pay and were being carried on an account.

In the years since the grocer died, Kenneth, often accompanied by his good wife, still visits the poorest part of the town and hands out gifts to all those who are in need.

Once the gentleman finished with the tale, he would produce a large bag and begin handing out gifts. In all those years, I cannot recall any outstretched hand coming away empty.

You may indeed say, "This is a very strange Christmas story," yet it happened just the same. Let me end this tale by simply saying, "Merry Christmas to one and all."

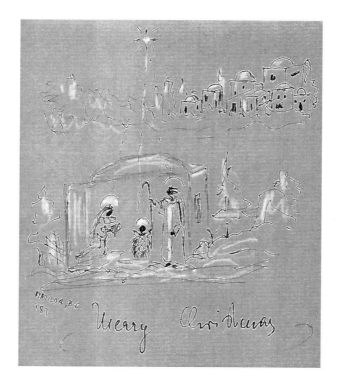

Anton Von Stefan grew up in Vancouver, Surrey, and Richmond, BC. After graduating from Vancouver College, he spent forty-two years working at the Pacific Grain Terminal on Vancouver's waterfront before retiring and becoming a full-time writer. Prior to his retirement, he spent several years as a freelance photographer and writer, contributing to the *Harold and Times* and the *City Drive News*, both local newspapers.

The author's first short story, *The Passing of Mr Needles*, was written in the summer of 1982. He has completed over thirty-seven short stories, of which were published by Granville Island Publishing in 2017 and can be found in his book *The Curse of The Red Crystal*.

He is in negotiations with a screenwriter to bring this book, *A Very Strange Christmas!*, to the stage . . .

You can read about the author and his works on his website:

www.antonvonstefan.com